T0247146

The Syrian Drummer and the Cactus Crimson Paint

PRAISE FOR *STORYSHARES*

"One of the brightest innovators and game-changers in the education industry."
– Forbes

"Your success in applying research-validated practices to promote literacy serves as a valuable model for other organizations seeking to create evidence-based literacy programs."

- Library of Congress

"We need powerful social and educational innovation, and Storyshares is breaking new ground. The organization addresses critical problems facing our students and teachers. I am excited about the strategies it brings to the collective work of making sure every student has an equal chance in life."
– Teach For America

"Around the world, this is one of the up-and-coming trailblazers changing the landscape of literacy and education."
- International Literacy Association

"It's the perfect idea. There's really nothing like this. I mean wow, this will be a wonderful experience for young people."   - Andrea Davis Pinkney, Executive Director, Scholastic

"Reading for meaning opens opportunities for a lifetime of learning. Providing emerging readers with engaging texts that are designed to offer both challenges and support for each individual will improve their lives for years to come. Storyshares is a wonderful start."
- David Rose, Co-founder of CAST & UDL

The Syrian Drummer and the Cactus Crimson Paint

Brian Kirchner

STORYSHARES

Story Share, Inc.
New York. Boston. Philadelphia

Storyshares
Story Share, Inc.
24 N. Bryn Mawr Avenue #340
Bryn Mawr, PA 19010-3304
www.storyshares.org

Inspiring reading with a new kind of book.

Interest Level: High School
Grade Level Equivalent: 3.3

9781973471073

Book design by Storyshares

Printed in the United States of America

Storyshares Presents

1

"Hey, if you guys see that new Syrian kid, you tell him I'm watching him, and he's gonna get deported!"

This came from Derek Bodley as he skulked up the driveway of my house to the garage, where I was practicing with my band, the People Movers. I say skulked because that's the best word for how Bodley moved. He was the kind of kid that always seemed to be trying to sneak up on people, instead of just walking up to them.

He was skinny, with a narrow face and a little bit of wispy hair on his upper lip that he called a mustache. He never looked you directly in the face, that was the oddest thing about him. He was always looking at you sidelong, with his face turned away a little bit. Bodley lived a few blocks away and was fifteen, the same age as we were. He spent most of his time wandering the neighborhood looking for trouble.

As usual, he was wearing his ill-fitting red baseball cap with his favorite political slogan printed on it. For some reason he had a pair of binoculars slung around his scrawny neck.

He stopped just short of the garage entrance, in the shade of a big elm tree growing in my front yard, and squinted at us. Late afternoon summer sunlight threw his shadow across the driveway.

Our singer, Xavier Montgomery Maplethorpe, whom everyone just called X, slouched with one arm draped over his mic stand. His stork-like, six-foot frame was topped by a huge ball of frizzy black hair. He regarded Derek with a cool gaze and a faint smile.

"Hey, man, the election was nine months ago, or didn't you hear? Why you still wearing that cap, fool? Thing's so ugly it's givin' me a migraine."

The rest of us laughed, the rest of us being me, Carlos Villareal on lead guitar, and Kenji Omura on bass. We were currently short a drummer.

We'd grown up together on the same block in Redford, Michigan, near Detroit. All of us went to Redford High School, where we'd be sophomores in the fall. Right now it was still summer, August 1st, and we had almost four glorious weeks of freedom left.

Derek glared at X out of the corner of one eye. "What'd you say?" he asked, in a sullen tone of voice. That was another thing about Bodley: he always sounded sullen, like he'd just been caught doing something wrong.

X leaned into the mic. "I said WHY ARE YOU STILL WEARING THAT DUMB CAP, FOOL?"

The amplifier stack against one wall blasted his voice out at maximum volume. Derek jumped and squawked, then his face went brick red. I laughed.

"You illegal beaner!" he said, pointing at me. "Your sorry butt's gonna get deported right back to Mexico, you'll see." He tapped the binoculars around his neck. "I'm watching. All the time."

I flashed the peace sign at him. *"Hasta la vista, amigo!"* I said in my best Speedy Gonzalez accent. It was the only Spanish I knew.

An old, blue Chevy pickup pulled up in front of my house, belching oil smoke from its rusty tailpipe. The engine revved and backfired.

"What're you doin' talkin' to them people?" yelled an older version of Derek from the driver's seat: Derek's dad, of course. Vince Bodley worked at the Woodhaven Stamping Plant and was even meaner than his offspring. A cigarette hung from his mouth. "Get in the truck, boy!"

Derek glowered at his dad. "I'm comin', Pop, just hold on, awright?" Then he turned back to us and said with a sneer, "Your band sucks, by the way. You ain't even got a drummer."

The elder Bodley let loose a stream of cursing that practically blistered the finish off my Fender guitar. He finished with, "Get your skinny butt in this truck, now!"

"Jet, you hot mess," said X to Derek. "Oh, by the way, bro, you have any luck stealing those comic books down at the Hobby House? I know you just came from there."

Derek frowned. "How'd you—"

"Never mind, my man. Go on, jet. Your daddy's waitin' on you."

Derek, at a loss for words, got into his dad's truck. They roared off in a cloud of smoke.

2

I had to admit that Bodley had a point about the drummer thing. Up until two weeks ago, a kid named Bilal Al-said had done skins duty for us, but his dad had moved their family back to Lebanon after the election. Here in southeast Michigan, with its big Arabic population, a lot of people were worried. And Bilal had been a pretty kick-butt drummer, too. Thank you, haters.

"What Syrian kid was he talking about?" I asked.

Kenji answered. "There's a family of refugees, they just moved in over on Hawthorn," he said.

"Oh yeah?" said X. "You meet them yet?"

"No. But my folks want to have them over for dinner soon, to welcome them to the neighborhood."

"Cool," said X.

"Dudes, we gotta hold drummer tryouts," I said.

"Solid," said X, nodding and making his huge Afro bounce. "Craigslist, baby."

"Hey, X," I said as I packed up my Fender. "How'd you know about the comic books?"

"Oh, that?" X shrugged. "Ain't no thing. His cap had blue paint dust on it. Right now Hobby House is sanding blue paint off their ceiling over the comic book rack. Got water-damaged up there or something. He was standing at the rack and it got all over his hat."

"But how'd you know he was trying to steal something? Maybe he was just looking."

"Then he was looking for a long time, brother. Lot of dust on that hat. Yeah, maybe he was just browsing. But Bodley? Uh-uh, I give you ten to one he was looking to get the five-finger discount."

Kenji shook his head. "X, someday you need to tell me how you do that."

"Like I said, ain't no thing." He grinned at us. "Let's go find us a skins man."

3

A few days later, we were back in the garage, trying to work our way through a cover of Crosstown Traffic. We didn't sound that good, to be honest, but X killed the vocals. He was a huge Hendrix fan. He even sounded like Hendrix when he sang.

When the last chords faded away, we all just stared at each other. Finally, Kenji spoke up and said what we were all thinking. "We need a drummer. Badly."

We all looked at the drum kit at the back of the garage, an old secondhand Ludwig with beat-up heads and a couple of dented Zildjian cymbals.

"Why'd that cat have to up and move?" said X, referring to our old drummer, Bilal. "That dude could lay down a beat."

We stood around the kit for a few minutes like mourners at a funeral.

"Excuse?" said a voice behind us in a Middle Eastern accent. "Drummer? Yes?"

We turned to see the owner of the voice.

It was a short, brown-skinned kid, smiling and holding a piece of paper. He was at least six inches shorter than me, and I'm not exactly tall. He wore bright orange gym shorts, socks up to his knees, blue Converse All-Stars, and a green Michigan State T-shirt. Best of all, on his head was a beat-up old straw cowboy hat with an American flag bandanna tied around it. It was the craziest outfit I'd ever seen. I liked him right away.

"Hey, dude, what's your name?" I asked.

"Yusuf," the kid said. "I am Yusuf Karout. I saw Craigslist. Drummer?" He held out the paper. X took it.

"It's the ad we posted," he said. He looked at Yusuf and smiled. "I'm X. These two fellas are Carlos and Kenji. You wanna try it out, brother?" He jerked his thumb at the drum kit.

Yusuf nodded rapidly. "Yes, yes, drums!" He mimicked playing with invisible drumsticks.

"All right, hit it, my man," said X.

"Thank you," said Yusuf, and sat down behind the kit. He snagged a pair of sticks from the floor.

Yusuf worked that kit like he was born to do it. We watched in growing amazement as he filled the garage with the most butt-kicking drum solo we'd ever seen outside of a Rush concert. The cowboy hat stayed perched on his head the whole time, too, like it was glued there. By the time Yusuf was done, he was sweating a river.

"I play band in Syria," he said.

"Oh, baby," said X, and laughed. "You owned that kit! You killed it! Syria, you said? Oh, you with that new family over on Hawthorn. Cool, bro."

"Dude, that totally rocked," I added. "Seriously."

Kenji was nodding. He looked at X and me. "I think we've got ourselves a drummer."

Yusuf stood up and shook hands with all of us. He had a strong grip. "Friends, thank you! I am very glad!" Then he checked his watch. "It is almost the praying time. Excuse?"

"Praying time?" said X.

"Yes," said Yusuf, stepping out from behind the kit. "Muslim." He pointed to himself. "Praying time."

X nodded. "Oh, yeah. Solid. Can you come back? We gotta hear more."

"Come back?" said Yusuf. "Yes, yes. We jam?"

"Oh, yeah, man, we jam," I said, clapping Yusuf on the shoulder. "We definitely jam."

Yusuf nodded happily and stepped out of the garage.

4

At that moment, Derek Bodley and his dumb red hat sidled up the sidewalk again. He stopped and stared at Yusuf.

"You ain't welcome here," he snarled. "Get out."

"It's my garage, Bodley," I said. "I say who stays and who goes. And I say he stays."

"Screw you, beaner. You're aiding and abetting an enemy of the United States. You're gonna get deported right along with your camel jockey buddy, here."

He crept slowly up the driveway, staring at the ground and throwing occasional stink-eyed glances at us, until he was standing right in front of Yusuf. Yusuf stood his ground. I stepped closer to them.

"Yeah, you know all about the new laws, right, camel jockey? The Make America Safe Again Act? It's the law of the land now. Just one screw up, and you're gone. No tolerance for criminal foreigners, that's how it works in America now."

Suddenly, Derek reached out and grabbed the cowboy hat from Yusuf's head. He reached inside it and started pulling straws out of the weave.

"Give that back to him, you moron," I said.

Derek grabbed a fistful of straw and pulled hard, tearing a chunk of the hat away and leaving a hole through one side.

"Sure," said Derek, and tossed the damaged hat at Yusuf. Yusuf picked it up and stared at the hole.

Just then, my dad stuck his head out the front door. "Derek Bodley?" he said, frowning. "Take a hike, Derek, before I call your old man. Stop causing trouble."

Bodley glared at my dad, but turned to leave. As he did, he gave us a parting shot. "Your sorry little camel jockey butt's getting deported, you'll see!" he yelled, then wandered off.

5

"So, what was it like? Getting to America? It must've been hella bad."

Kenji kicked me under the table and glared at me.

I mouthed "What?" at him.

Mr. Karout spooned more hummus onto his plate. He looked serious, but not angry. Mrs. Karout looked sad.

"Sorry, Mr. Karout," said Kenji. "My friend here doesn't have any manners."

"There is no need to apologize, Kenji," said Mr. Karout. "It is a natural question. We don't mind."

It was a week after we'd met Yusuf, and we were all sitting in the Karout's tiny two-room apartment a few blocks from my house. Yusuf had come to our practice that day and invited us for dinner afterward.

"Carlos, Kenji, Xavier, come with me," said Mrs. Karout. "I want to show you something."

She got up from the table. She was wearing a black headscarf and she wrapped it more tightly around her face.

She led us into the other room and opened the closet. She took out a small life jacket. It was faded orange, torn, with patches of greenish stuff, like mold. A wrinkled picture of a little girl was pinned to it.

"This is the life jacket my daughter, Rima, was wearing when she died," Mrs. Karout said. "She was five years old. This is the only picture of her we have. It was taken at her last birthday."

The girl had dark, curly hair and a smile like Yusuf's. She was holding a bunch of balloons.

The colors in the photo were faded but I could see the balloons were purple.

Mrs. Karout said, "Rima's favorite color was purple. She insisted that everything at her birthday party be purple."

I stared at the photo of the smiling little girl and the mossy life jacket. She looked like any other kid. She looked like anyone at my old elementary school, except that she was wearing different clothes.

"Rima fell out of our little boat as we crossed the Mediterranean Sea," said Mrs. Karout. "We tried to get her back in, but we couldn't. My husband even jumped in, too. He almost drowned himself, but the other passengers saved him. But Rima... we never saw her again. All Hussein could find was her life jacket." She paused, and wiped a single tear from her cheek. "But one day she will welcome her family to paradise, in shallah. She paused for a moment, looking at the picture, then continued. "You've heard of the MASA Act?"

I nodded. "Yeah. Make America Safe Again. Stupid law."

"A dangerous law," said Mrs. Karout. "One legal infraction, no matter how small, committed by any family member means deportation for all. Even a parking ticket. And then where would we go? Our native Syria is in ruins. We would be without a country. Worst of all, Rima's death would have been for nothing."

We were silent, even X, who always had something to say.

"In spite of this, we are very grateful to have reached America," she continued. "And we are thankful for the friendship you have extended to Yusuf. He has been so lonely since we lost his sister. It means more to us than you can imagine."

X was the first one to find his voice again. "Much respect, Mrs. K, much respect," he said quietly. "Am I right, fellas?"

Kenji and I nodded. "Much respect."

6

On Saturday afternoon, August 16th , X, Kenji, and I were hanging out in the garage, waiting for Yusuf so we could start practice. It was 5:00, and we'd been there about a half-hour when he came up the driveway holding a new pair of drumsticks. He showed them to us proudly. They were spray-painted red, white, and blue.

"Niiiiice!" said X. "You do this yourself?"

Yusuf nodded. "I do it yesterday."

"That's a weird shade of red," Kenji pointed out. He was right. The red had a lot of orange in it.

"Is Cactus Crimson," said Yusuf. "I borrow paint from neighbor. Artist lady. Nice."

"You mean Miz Hendrickson?" X said. "Yeah, she cool, she funky."

We all knew Linda Hendrickson. She was an aging hippie artist who lived alone next to the Karouts' apartment building.

"Cactus Crimson?" I said. "That's killer, Yusuf. Dude, you ready to bang it?"

Yusuf nodded and gave a thumbs-up, then got behind the kit. "We play Start Me Up?" he said. "Rolling Stones? Yes?"

"You got it, baby," said X, taking his place at the mic.

I started the intro guitar riff, then stopped dead when Yusuf's dad came walking up the driveway. There were two cops with him.

"What's up with this?" I said.

Mr. Karout spoke to Yusuf in Arabic. Yusuf got pale, and shook his head, but he got up from behind the drums and went out to where his dad was.

"Yusuf has to go home now," Mr. Karout told us. "I'm sorry. These policemen need to talk to him. Goodbye."

He turned and left with Yusuf in tow. The cops followed. Yusuf looked back at us, scared.

Kenji whistled between his teeth. "Not cool."

X shook his head, making his fluffy Afro bounce. "Nope. Maybe my pops knows something."

7

The following Monday, Kenji and I met X at his house, and we all sat in the small living room.

X's dad was a detective with the Redford Police Department. He'd been shot in the leg on the job and only worked part-time now, but kept in touch with his contacts on the force. He sometimes gave X the lowdown on interesting cases. The living room walls were decorated with framed medals and citations recording Detective Monty Maplethorpe's career.

The man himself sat in one corner, leaned back in his old, cracked, red leather recliner, smoking a big cigar.

His bad leg was propped up on the edge of an ottoman made of the same red leather.

"Pops," X began.

"I know, I know, boy. You want to know all about the Karout thing." He puffed out foul smoke and regarded us with a raised eyebrow.

X nodded. "You got it, Pops. You got the 411?"

Detective Maplethorpe chuckled. It sounded like a bullfrog laughing. "Sure I do. Talked to my buddy Rintz just this mornin'. Figured you boys'd be stopping by."

Kenji said, "What did you find out?"

"Graffiti was discovered on the Bodley's garage last Saturday morning. Spray paint. Those officers wanted to talk to your friend about it."

"What kind of graffiti?" I asked. "Why Yusuf? Why'd they think he might be involved?"

The detective grunted around his cigar. "That's the lousy part, Carlos. It says *infidels must die*."

Suddenly it seemed like all the oxygen had been sucked out of the room.

"So of course the first person they pick on is the Muslim kid," said X in disgust. "Typical!"

"Hold on, Xavier. Don't go jumpin' to conclusions. They just wanted to interview the kid. He wasn't arrested. And they went to him because the homeowner claimed to have seen him on the property the night before with a can of spray paint."

"Bullcrap!" said X. "The homeowner? You mean Vince Bodley? He hates Yusuf's family."

"Did your guy tell you anything else?" asked Kenji.

"Yeah, he did. Now, what I'm gonna tell you doesn't leave this room. Understood?"

We all nodded.

"A hair was found stuck in the paint. DNA from it matches Yusuf's."

"No way," I said. "Impossible."

"Just tellin' you what I was told."

X looked worried. "They could get deported, Pops."

The detective nodded. "Under the MASA Act, I'm afraid so. If Yusuf is found guilty." He sounded unhappy about it. "My gut tells me he didn't do it. But we gotta go by the evidence."

He didn't have anything else to tell us, so we left. We wandered down the street toward my house. Late afternoon summer sun lit up the trees.

"Doesnt look good," said Kenji. "That DNA match sounds solid."

"Yeah. Pretty solid," X muttered to himself. Then, to Kenji and me: "We need to visit the scene of the crime, fellas."

"Bodley's house?" I asked.

"Right on," he said. We headed in that direction.

8

"That little punk terrorist did it! It was him!" Derek Bodley sat on his crumbling front porch with a nasty little grin on his narrow face. As usual, his red hat was perched on his head.

Kenji, X, and I stood down at the end of the driveway, staring.

There it was. Spray-painted in reddish-orange letters across the garage door were the words Detective Maplethorpe had told us about:

INFIDELS MUST DIE!

The letters were low, only about five feet and change from the ground. X whipped out his phone and snapped a pic of the paint.

"Put that away," said Derek.

"Public sidewalk, man, it's legal," said X without looking at Derek. He was peering at the picture. Then he walked up to Derek and grabbed the red hat from his head.

"Hey!" Derek yelled. "Gimme that!" Even when he yelled, the dude sounded like he was pouting.

X ignored him, instead inspecting the hat carefully, holding it close to his face. Then he snapped a picture of the hat and tossed it back at Derek.

"Bodley, my man," said X as he walked back toward Kenji and me. "Yusuf didn't do it. We know he didn't do it. And we're gonna prove he didn't do it. You dig?"

Derek's grin faltered a little, but we felt his hostile stare on our backs as we walked away.

After a couple of blocks, Kenji asked the obvious question. "X, how do you know Derek did it? And what was up with those pics?"

"No time, brothers," said X. He was walking quickly. "I'll explain later. Right now we gotta hit Hendrickson's."

"Hippie Hendrickson? The painter who loaned Yusuf the Cactus Crimson?" said Koji.

"Right on, baby."

9

Twenty minutes later, we were standing in Linda Hendrickson's backyard, a cluttered graveyard of half-finished sculptures and gardening tools. Hendrickson herself was a tall, thin, middle-aged woman who wore billowy, colorful clothes and Birkenstock sandals.

"You want to see the paint shed?" she asked.

"Yeah, Miz H, if you don't mind," said X.

"No, not at all. If it might help that new Syrian family." She blinked rapidly and her eyes took on a misty look. "Those poor people, the world is an unjust place."

We went to the shed, a tiny shack at the back of the property. There was a small garden in front of it. X stopped, knelt down and pinched some soil between his fingers.

"Sticky," he muttered.

Then he got up and looked into the paint shed. Just inside the doorway was a shelf full of spray paint cans. Right in front was a can with the words *Cactus Crimson* on it.

I was about to step inside, but X said, "Jump back, bro. Not yet."

I stepped back and gave X some room. He got down on his hands and knees and examined the shed's wood floor. It was covered in a thin layer of brown dust with footprints in it. X put his nose almost to the floor and sniffed.

"Is this fertilizer, Miz H?" he asked.

"Oh, yes, I spilled some in there last Thursday and haven't had time to clean it up."

"That was Thursday the 14th?"

"Yes."

"Who's been in this shed recently besides you?"

"Well, Yusuf was in there, and then a cop on Saturday getting fingerprints from the can."

"Fingerprints!" I said. "Bodley's nailed!"

"Nope," said X. "Bet he wore gloves. Cops ain't gonna find anyone's prints except Yusufs and Miz H's. But it ain't no thing. We got something better. Miz H, do you still have the bag of fertilizer you spilled?"

"Sure," she said, and grabbed a burlap sack from behind the shed. It was empty, and had a small tear in one side. "Such a shame. It wasn't cheap."

"I bet," said X, studying the bag. "From Thailand?"

"Yes! How did you know?"

He pointed to the label. It was written in an exotic script. "This is Thai writing. Can I keep this bag?"

"Sure you can."

"Thanks. What about that garden? You mix clay in that soil, right?"

"Yes," she said. "It helps the soil retain moisture."

"Right on, right on. All right, Miz H. I think that's it. You've done us a solid, and the Karouts, too. For real."

"Well, okay, then, I'm glad to be able to help." She looked mystified. "That is, if I did help."

Xavier waved at her. He was halfway across the backyard already, on his way back to the street. "You sure did, Miz H. You have no idea."

10

"How did you know about that Thai writing?" Kenji asked as we left.

We were passing the small apartment building where the Karouts lived. There was a light on in their second-floor window. I knew they had to be worried.

"Learning foreign alphabets is a hobby of mine, you dig?" said X.

Suddenly the front door of the apartment building flew open, and Yusuf ran out. He came over to us, out of breath. "My father, my father," he said, struggling to find the English words. "Police!" He brought his wrists together.

"Handcuffs?" said X. "Your dad got arrested?"

Yusuf nodded angrily. "Yes, yes! Arrested! Because paint. Police believe I paint. So they arrest my father. Two hours ago." He spat on the ground. "We have done nothing wrong. Nothing!"

Kenji cursed. I felt helpless. X looked thoughtful.

"Will they deport?" said Yusuf.

X grabbed Yusuf by the shoulders. "My brother, hear this. Your family is not gettin' deported. Do you read me, brother? You got my promise."

Yusuf looked skeptical. "I hope you can help us, but what can you do?"

X threw back his giant Afro and laughed out loud. "You leave that to us, bro. Your family ain't goin' nowhere. You know why? Cause ain't nobody takin' our new drummer, that's why, baby!"

Yusuf gave X a small smile. "Okay, X. I hope you are correct. I have to go now. Goodbye, my friends." Then he went back into his building.

"X, what's up with that, dude?" I said a few minutes later. We were almost to my house. "I hope you have something brewing under that Afro."

"We got everything we need." He patted the fertilizer bag from Hendrickson's and then the pocket carrying his phone. "My soul brothers, we are gonna get Yusuf off the hook, and hang Derek Bodley on it instead." It was getting dark. "You fellas jet home. I gotta talk to my Pops."

11

The next day, after dinner, the four of us were lounging in our practice space. Yusuf was grinning big enough to split his face open. His father had been released earlier in the day.

"How did you do it, X?" asked Yusuf. "My dad is home again, and the police have even apologized to my family!"

"Ain't no thing, bro," said X. "Bodley tried to frame you. He tagged his own garage with that graffiti, man." He took out his phone and pulled up the pic he'd snapped of the graffiti and held it up for all of us to see.

"See how the letters are smeared downward a little? And the overspray from the paint stream... its all below the letters, never above em."

I saw what he meant. The letters were a little distorted, as if the spray had hit the garage at an angle instead of straight on. And the tiny droplets of overspray were all spread out below the letters.

"It looks like someone tall was spraying downward," said Kenji.

"To get the letters lower on the door," I added, and looked at Yusuf. "Maybe so it looked like a short guy did it."

Yusuf nodded.

"Right on," said X. "Next pic."

He swiped, and the picture of Derek Bodley's hat appeared. He zoomed it in.

"What are all of these tiny dots all over the hat?" asked Yusuf, peering closely at the photo.

"Paint dots," said X. "Cactus Crimson paint. He was wearing his hat while he was spraying."

"But, what about the hair?" Yusuf pointed out. The DNA matched.

"Course it did, 'cause it was your hair. Planted by Bodley, of course. Remember when he grabbed your cowboy hat?"

"Oh man," Kenji whispered. "He got some hairs out of it."

Yusuf removed his hat and stared at the hole Bodley had torn in it. "Derek Bodley is really a jerkhead."

X grinned and nodded. "Jerkhead, right on. Probably started thinkin' of ways to get you and your fam booted out as soon as he saw you move in."

"Why'd you need to visit Hendrickson?" asked Kenji.

"The DNA match was too strong and the paint evidence was too weak," said X. "I needed something that would tie Bodley to the paint can."

"The footprints in the shed," I said.

"Nope. They were too messed up. Useless. But that Thai fertilizer, now that was solid, brothers."

"Anyone who went into that shed after Hendrickson spilled the fertilizer got it all over their shoes," I said.

"Right," said X. "But there was a problem. That powder was dry, wouldn't have stayed on anyone's shoes for long."

"The garden," Kenji said.

"Right on. Footprint. It was faint, no good for an ID, but it was too big to be Yusuf's or Miz H's. That left the cop who pulled prints from the can, or Bodley."

"Anyone who stepped in that clay and then the fertilizer would still have fertilizer on his shoes," I finished.

"Right. I told my pops everything. He worked the phone until he got a judge to sign off on a search warrant. The cops went to Bodley's house yesterday and grabbed his shoes. There was mud on the bottom. They tested it. Guess what they found?"

"Fertilizer from Thailand," Kenji and I said in unison.

"Sure did. They took the paint can into the lab and got some DNA off of it. I dont know how, but they did. Some of the DNA matched Bodley's. That sealed the deal."

Kenji spoke up. "So Bodley snuck over to Hendrickson's sometime on the night of Friday the 15th , stole the same paint can he knew Yusuf had used for his sticks, and painted terrorist graffiti on his own garage to frame Yusuf and get his family deported. Is that about right?"

"Right as right can be, brother," said X.

"But why'd Bodley care what kind of paint he used?" I asked. "Also, how'd Bodley know what kind of paint Yusuf used on his sticks?"

"Oh yeah, I forgot," said X. "You're right on, it didn't really matter what kind of paint he used. I guess he wanted to make extra sure the blame got put on Yusuf. And how'd he know what paint to use? Remember when he came to our practice that first time? He had binoculars. He saw Yusuf go over to Hendrickson's and come back with that paint."

Yusuf gave X a fist bump. "You are the bomb! You saved my family."

"Ain't no thing, man," said X. "Can't let a drummer with mad skills like you got get away." He checked his phone. "Almost time."

"For what?" said Kenji.

"My dad told me the cops would be hitting Bodley's place in about half an hour. I wanna go see."

"But he can't be arrested for vandalizing his own house," I pointed out.

"Nope. But the cops are gonna give his dad the 411 about him spraying his own garage. And that, my brothers, is something we do not want to miss."

Yusuf nodded and gave a thumbs-up. "I can't wait to see this!" he said. "But first, let's jam." He slapped his funky hat back on his head and pulled his Cactus Crimson sticks out of a back pocket.

Five minutes later, we were cranking out Crosstown Traffic. This time, with Yusuf laying down a beat, we sounded like pure gold.

About The Author

Brian Kirchner teaches Geology at Henry Ford College, near Detroit, Michigan. He lives in Royal Oak, Michigan with his wife and three kids. Brian has loved writing fiction since a very young age, but took a (very) long hiatus from it while earning a doctorate in Geology and starting a family. Since taking up writing again in 2016, Brian has published a short story in the online literary magazine "Inklette," was awarded 9th place in a Writer's Digest international poetry competition, and has published a short humor piece at the online site "Funny in Five Hundred." Brian has also written a novel and is currently shopping it around to literary agencies.

Besides writing and teaching about rocks, Brian enjoys playing guitar and banjo, reading (just about anything), road trips, astronomy, and pizza.

About The Publisher

Story Shares is a nonprofit focused on supporting the
millions of teens and adults who struggle with reading by
creating a new shelf in the library specifically for them. The
ever-growing collection features content that is compelling and
culturally relevant for teens and adults, yet still readable at a
range of lower reading levels.

Story Shares generates content by engaging deeply with
writers, bringing together a community to create this new kind
of book. With more intriguing and approachable stories to
choose from, the teens and adults who have fallen behind are
improving their skills and beginning to discover the joy of
reading. For more information, visit storyshares.org.

Easy to Read. Hard to Put Down.

Made in the USA
Middletown, DE
20 January 2023